Anna & Solomon

Elaine Snyder

Pictures by Harry Bliss

Name: Solomon Friedman
Sailing Date: April 24, 1898
To: New York, USA

Margaret Ferguson Books

FARRAR STRAUS GIROUX

New York

Once—and not once upon a time, because this is a true story—in
1897 in Russia there lived a handsome young man who fell in
love with a beautiful young woman, and one bright day,
under a canopy of leaves and spring flowers, they were married.
His name was Solomon and her name was Anna, and they lived in
the Jewish quarter in the town of Vitebsk.

Vitebsk was well-known as the home of many merchants, craftsmen, and artists. A number of the artists were Jewish. Like them, Solomon was a painter, but he did not paint pictures; he painted houses. Mostly, he made dingy walls fresh and white.

But now and then, he would take sponges or old rags and deftly dab colorful patches of paint on a wall or he would make a plain wall look like the marble side of a courtly building. Anna and her family admired his work, and Solomon, who had no family, took pleasure in the kind praise of his new relatives.

Anna, too, was talented. She could add up long columns of numbers as quickly as she could braid up her long hair. Addition was a skill she had learned as a child from her father when he was still alive. Solomon would marvel at both the speed of her fingers and the quickness of her mind. "She is pure and perfect," he said to himself, "like the look of creamy paint when you first remove the lid from the can."

Shortly after Anna and Solomon's marriage, a calamity befell the Jews of Vitebsk. The ruler of the land, called the Czar, sent his soldiers on horses to the streets where the Jews lived. The soldiers entered their homes, broke their windows and furniture, stole their brass candlesticks, and destroyed their holy books.

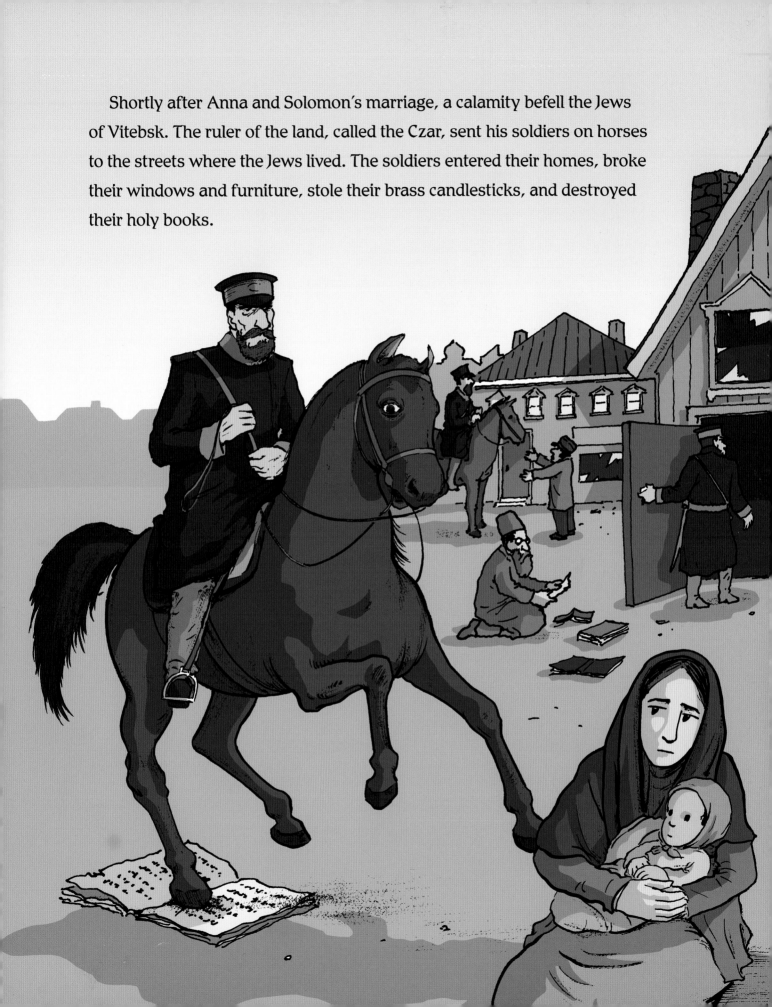

Solomon decided that he no longer wanted to live in a place where his people were persecuted and harm might come to Anna. He had heard of a country across the ocean where one could live without fear and could prosper . . . the United States of America. But what was he to do? He had little money, and money was needed to get there.

He and Anna put their heads together and Anna's quick mind came up with a plan. "Solomon," she declared, "you must go alone. We have just enough money to buy one passage to the new country."

Anna looked into her husband's tender eyes and stroked his cheeks as she explained. She would stay behind with her family in a small village outside of Vitebsk which had not been ransacked by the Czar's soldiers. With her talent for numbers she could find work in the local produce market. Standing by a scale with pencil and pad she would weigh the fruit and vegetables and add up the prices. As soon as Solomon could save enough money painting houses in America, he was to send for her, and she'd come to him with her crown of braided hair, her crisp cotton blouses, her songs and smiles, and they would start a family.

There he found a room to rent in the lower east side of the city,
where many other immigrants lived.

Once settled, Solomon worked very hard. Each day he put on overalls and shoes spattered with paint, climbed ladders, scraped, plastered, and painted walls, and, at the end of the day, cleaned his brushes.

On the Sabbath, he rested
and went to synagogue. The
synagogue, a store that had been
converted into a house of prayer,
was small and crowded. Here
Solomon prayed for Anna and
their reunion.

Many months went by, many walls were plastered, many rooms were painted, and, at last, Solomon had earned enough to send for his bride.

Off he ran to the post office to send her money for the fare. Anna quickly wrote back, letting him know the date of the ship's arrival.

When the day came, Solomon went to the pier full of excitement, carrying flowers and a potted snake plant tucked under his arm.

He searched amid the crowd . . .

He inquired . . .

He began to worry . . .

As Solomon watched the last person leave the ship, it dawned on him . . .

Anna wasn't going to walk down the ramp. But there was Label!

Label was Anna's youngest brother. He was small and skinny, and Solomon remembered how protective Anna had always been of him. Why was he here? Where was Anna?

Label carefully explained to him that Anna had used the money Solomon sent not for herself but for her brother's passage instead.

Oy, oy, it was a great blow to Solomon, but he saw that Anna was right. Label could not be left behind; Anna had to be certain that he would be safe.

Solomon took Label home.

That evening, while Solomon sliced up salami and bread, he listened to Label's stories about Anna. Label told him how she bustled around the market all day, often bringing potatoes and greens back to the family, and how very much she missed her husband. But it was Label's report that the village outside of Vitebsk remained untouched by the Czar's soldiers that meant the most to Solomon.

It wasn't long before Label joined Solomon painting houses. Word soon spread of their skill, speed, and low prices. Before long, the two painters were working night and day.

Months passed, summer became fall, winter came again, and Solomon had once more earned enough money to send for Anna.

Solomon waited with anticipation for the day of the ship's arrival, and when
it came, he went to the pier to meet his bride.

He searched amid the crowd . . .

He inquired . . .

He began to worry . . .

Then he spotted a familiar face. Was it Anna's?

No—not unless Anna had grown whiskers on her chin!

It was her older brother, Velvul, who trotted down the gangplank with his cardboard suitcase and his sparse, spiky beard.

Oh, Anna, Solomon thought, *how could you?*

What could Solomon do but take Velvul home with him. He understood that Anna was giving this brother an opportunity in the new world, too.

At first, Velvul worked with Solomon and Label painting houses, but after a while he was able to start a business of his own, selling herring from a cart and pickles from a barrel.

More months went by, and again Solomon had earned enough money to send for Anna.

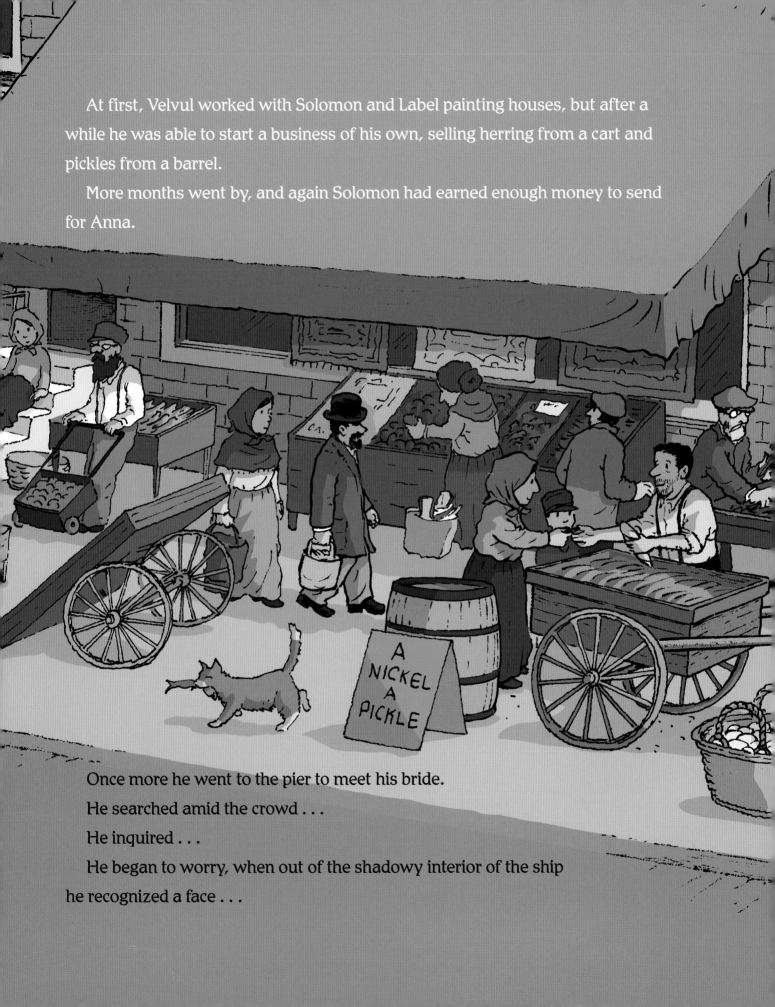

A
NICKEL
A
PICKLE

Once more he went to the pier to meet his bride.

He searched amid the crowd . . .

He inquired . . .

He began to worry, when out of the shadowy interior of the ship he recognized a face . . .

It was Anna's mother.

Solomon was deeply disappointed, but his heart soon softened. "Could Anna leave her old mother behind? Of course not," he said to himself, and bravely took her home.

Home was now a three-room walk-up that included two adopted cats, Mischa and Pischa, both of whom loved herring and an occasional pickle. Anna's mother was a wonderful cook. She prepared dishes of borscht and dumplings for the men, and that made Solomon miss Anna all the more.

Time passed, winter became spring, and once again Solomon went to the pier to meet his beloved Anna. Was his bride on the ship? A melancholy thought crossed his mind. After all, Anna had a sister, Mushka.

He searched amid the crowd . . .

He inquired . . .

But this time . . .

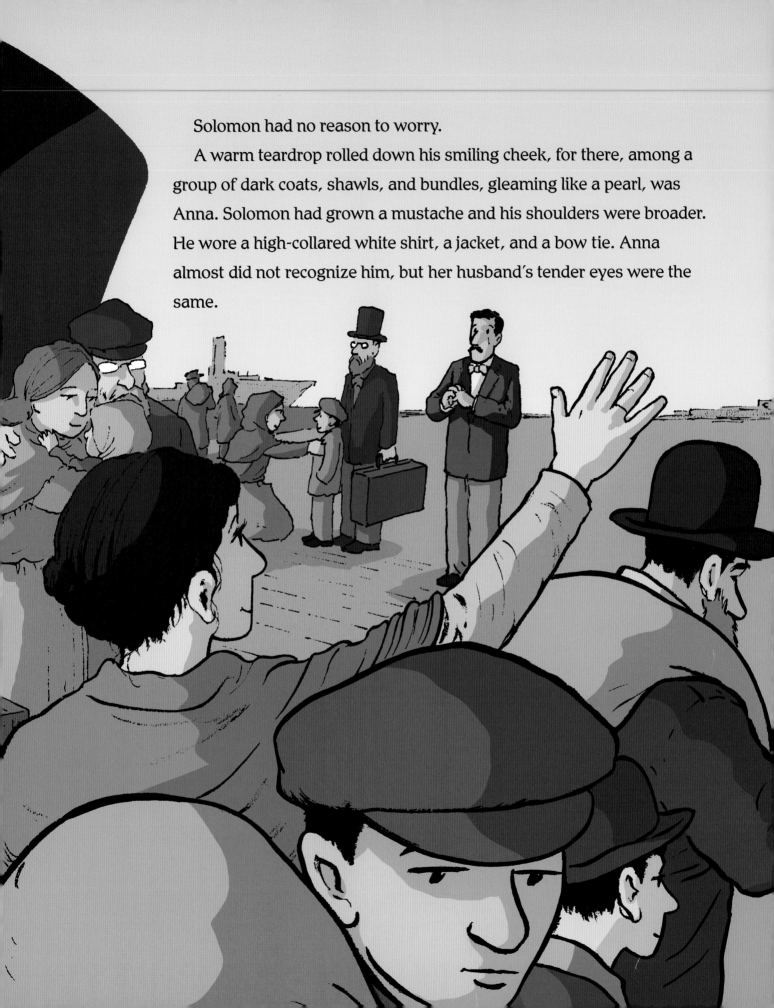

Solomon had no reason to worry.

A warm teardrop rolled down his smiling cheek, for there, among a group of dark coats, shawls, and bundles, gleaming like a pearl, was Anna. Solomon had grown a mustache and his shoulders were broader. He wore a high-collared white shirt, a jacket, and a bow tie. Anna almost did not recognize him, but her husband's tender eyes were the same.

They hugged with happiness. Finally,
Solomon and Anna were reunited.

Anna's sister would soon follow her to America. Velvul had written Anna that she should come because he was saving his money to buy a ticket for Mushka's passage. His business was doing well—the herring were flying off the cart and the pickles were jumping out of the barrel. It would be a good surprise for the overburdened Solomon, he proudly wrote.

Solomon took Anna home to an apartment of their own, rooms on the top floor.

In preparation for her arrival, he had painted all the walls with clusters of colossal flowers.

That spring, many pots of snake plants filled the windows, and before long a baby girl was born. Her name was Edna. The next year a boy was born. His name was David. Sarah and Frieda soon followed. Solomon and Anna's dreams had come true—they had their family in a land of freedom and liberty at last!

Author's Note

My grandparents were Anna and Solomon in this story, and my mother, Edna, was their first child. We lived a few blocks from my grandparents in Brooklyn, New York, and I have wonderful memories of my visits with them. Solomon went on to own several retail store properties in Brooklyn, but he continued to paint our apartment every spring to "freshen" it up. Down the street from their house, Anna had a candy store, which was frequented by children who attended P.S. 149 across the street. How Anna and her family arrived in America has become a family legend as the story is passed from generation to generation.

Anna and Solomon

Anna and Solomon in front of their candy store

Anna and Solomon with Edna

For Delia, Ruby, Amari, and
Alia, great-great-grandchildren
of Anna and Solomon
—E.S.

For Robert Dillof
—H.B.

Farrar Straus Giroux Books for Young Readers
175 Fifth Avenue, New York 10010

Text copyright © 2014 by Elaine Snyder
Pictures copyright © 2014 by Harry Bliss
All rights reserved
Color separations by Embassy Graphics Ltd.
Printed in China by Macmillan Production (Asia) Ltd.,
Kowloon Bay, Hong Kong (supplier code PS)
Designed by Andrew Arnold
First edition, 2014
1 3 5 7 9 10 8 6 4 2

mackids.com

Library of Congress Cataloging-in-Publication Data
Snyder, Elaine, author.
    Anna and Solomon / Elaine Snyder ; pictures by Harry Bliss.
        pages   cm
    "Margaret Ferguson Books."
    ISBN 978-0-374-30362-4 (hardcover)
    1. Jews—Belarus—Vitsebsk—Biography—Juvenile literature.   2. United
States—Emigration and immigration—Juvenile literature.   3. Snyder family.
4. Vitsebsk (Belarus)—Biography.   I. Bliss, Harry, 1964–   illustrator.
II. Title.

PZ7.S6851755An 2014

                                                                    2013007872

Farrar Straus Giroux Books for Young Readers may be purchased for business or promotional use.
For information on bulk purchases please contact Macmillan Corporate and Premium Sales Department at
(800) 221-7945 x5442 or by email at specialmarkets@macmillan.com.